THIS BOOK BELONGS TO:

TO ALL THE COOL KIDS.
– BIRDY

MISTER COOL
PUBLISHED IN THE UNITED STATES BY POW! A DIVISION OF POWERHOUSE PACKAGING & SUPPLY, INC.
TEXT © 2015 BIRDY JONES, ILLUSTRATIONS @ 2015 TARA D. LYNCH

ISBN 978-157687-719-7
LIBRARY OF CONGRESS CONTROL NUMBER: 2014937059
POWERHOUSE PACKAGING & SUPPLY, INC.
37 MAIN STREET, BROOKLYN, NY 11201-1021
INFO@POWKIDSBOOKS.COM, WWW.POWKIDSBOOKS.COM, WWW.POWERHOUSEBOOKS.COM, WWW.POWERHOUSEPACKAGING.COM
FIRST EDITION, 2015
BOOK DESIGN BY TARA D. LYNCH
10 9 8 7 6 5 4 3 2 1
PRINTED IN CHINA

MISTER COOL

BY BIRDY JONES · ILLUSTRATED BY TARA D. LYNCH

POW!

BROOKLYN, NY

BUT I'M *meter*

MISTER

COOL

NOT BECAUSE I CAN WALK ON MY HANDS

BACKWARDS
(BECAUSE I CAN)

NOT BECAUSE I CAN BOWL A

PERFECT GAME

GRANNY-
STYLE

(BECAUSE I HAVE)

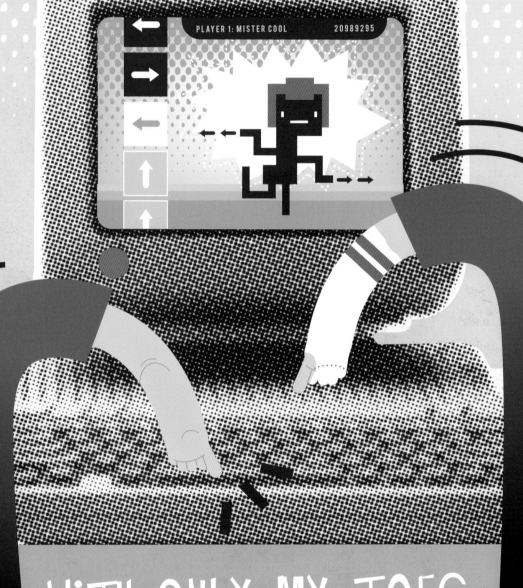

THEY CALL ME MISTER COOL
BECAUSE OF MY
SUPER
COOL
-OSiTY.

DANCE MOVES

BUT

GUESS

WHAT?!

THAT RUMOR IS **NOT** TRUE.

SOMETIMES,

ONE TIME THIS DUDE TRIPPED ME.

I GUESS HE COULDN'T HANDLE MY
COOLNESS.

HE SAID HE'D NEVER SEEN
A HEAD SPIN THAT
COOL.
HE SAID IT WAS PURE ART.

HE DITCHED TRIPPING, TOOK UP

BEAT-BOXING,

AND THANKED ME DURING HIS RECITAL.

I TOLD HER DWEEBS MAKE UP
90% OF THE WORLD

NOT DWEEBS

DWEEBS

AND WITH NUMBERS THAT LARGE,
SHE WAS PROBABLY ONE, TOO.

IT WAS NO SUPRISE TO FIND A LOVE♥LETTER ON MY DESK ON TUESDAY. IT READ,

"I GOT AN A. WILL YOU BE MY ❀NUMBER 1?"

ONE TIME THIS FELLA SPAT GUM
INTO MY HAIR.

(ACTUAL)
WRAPPER

— I'LL SAVE
THIS FOR LATER!

HE MUST'VE BEEN JEALOUS OF
MY MOHAWK.

I YANKED IT OUT

AND TWISTED UNTIL IT RESEMBLED

A BIRD IN FLIGHT.

He WENT ON TO WiN FiRST PLACE iN THE ART FAiR WiTH HiS SCULPTURE,

"THE LiNT BALL LiON".

"CAN COOLNESS BE BROKEN DOWN SCIENTIFICALLY AND MAINTAINED THROUGH SPACE AND TIME?"
"HOW CAN I BECOME JUST AS COOL AS YOU?"

AND i SAY,

SORRY!

I CAN'T TELL

YOU THAT!

BUT i CAN GiVE YOU A HiNT:

THE END.

MAKE YOUR OWN COOL CHARACTERS!

4/2017